THE
WORLD
DOESN'T
END

BOOKS BY CHARLES SIMIC

Charles Simic

THE WORLD DOESN'T END

PROSE POEMS

ecco

An Imprint of HarperCollinsPublishers

ecco

An Imprint of HarperCollins Publishers, registered in the United States of America
and/or other jurisdictions.

Some of these pieces have previously appeared in the following
magazines: to whose editors the author is grateful:
Pequod, Caliban, Western Humanities Review,
New American Writing, O-Blëk, Tri-Quarterly,
New Directions Annual, Five Fingers Review.

Library of Congress Cataloging-in-Publication Data
Simic, Charles, 1938–
The world doesn't end; prose poems/Charles Simic.—1st ed.
p.   cm.
ISBN 0-15-698350-8 (pbk.)
I. Title. II. Title: World doesn't end.
PS3569.I4725W67   1989
811'.54—dc19   88-21128

Design by Beth Tondreau Design/Jane Treuhaft
Type set in Sabon

Printed in the United States of America
22 23 24 25 26 LBC 7 6 5 4 3

for Jim Tate

CONTENTS

PART I

PART II

vii

PART III

"Let's waltz the rumba."
—Fats Waller

PART I

PART 1

My mother was a braid of black smoke.

She bore me swaddled over the burning cities.

The sky was a vast and windy place for a child to play.

We met many others who were just like us. They were trying to put on their overcoats with arms made of smoke.

The high heavens were full of little shrunken deaf ears instead of stars.

Scaliger turns deadly pale at the sight of watercress. Tycho Brahe, the famous astronomer, passes out at the sight of a caged fox. Maria de Medici feels instantly giddy on seeing a rose, even in a painting. My ancestors, meanwhile, are eating cabbage. They keep stirring the pot looking for a pigfoot which isn't there. The sky is blue. The nightingale sings in a Renaissance sonnet, and immediately someone goes to bed with a toothache.

I was stolen by the gypsies. My parents stole
me right back. Then the gypsies stole me again.
This went on for some time. One minute I was
in the caravan suckling the dark teat of my new
mother, the next I sat at the long dining room table
eating my breakfast with a silver spoon.

It was the first day of spring. One of my
fathers was singing in the bathtub; the other one
was painting a live sparrow the colors of a tropical
bird.

It's a store that specializes in antique porcelain. She goes around it with a finger on her lips. Tsss! We must be quiet when we come near the tea cups. Not a breath allowed near the sugar bowls. A teeny grain of dust has fallen on a wafer-thin saucer. She makes an "oh" with her owlet-mouth. On her feet she wears soft, thickly padded slippers around which mice scurry.

She's pressing me gently with a hot steam iron, or she slips her hand inside me as if I were a sock that needed mending. The thread she uses is like the trickle of my blood, but the needle's sharpness is all her own.

"You will ruin your eyes, Henrietta, in such bad light," her mother warns. And she's right! Never since the beginning of the world has there been so little light. Our winter afternoons have been known at times to last a hundred years.

We were so poor I had to take the place of the
bait in the mousetrap. All alone in the cellar, I
could hear them pacing upstairs, tossing and turn-
ing in their beds. "These are dark and evil days,"
the mouse told me as he nibbled my ear. Years
passed. My mother wore a cat-fur collar which
she stroked until its sparks lit up the cellar.

I am the last Napoleonic soldier. It's almost
two hundred years later and I am still retreating
from Moscow. The road is lined with white birch
trees and the mud comes up to my knees. The one-
eyed woman wants to sell me a chicken, and I don't
even have any clothes on.

The Germans are going one way; I am going
the other. The Russians are going still another way
and waving good-by. I have a ceremonial saber.
I use it to cut my hair, which is four feet long.

"Everybody knows the story about me and Dr. Freud," says my grandfather.

"We were in love with the same pair of black shoes in the window of the same shoe store. The store, unfortunately, was always closed. There'd be a sign: DEATH IN THE FAMILY or BACK AFTER LUNCH, but no matter how long I waited, no one would come to open.

"Once I caught Dr. Freud there shamelessly admiring the shoes. We glared at each other before going our separate ways, never to meet again."

He held the Beast of the Apocalypse by its tail, the stupid kid! Oh beards on fire, our doom appeared sealed. The buildings were tottering; the computer screens were as dark as our grandmother's cupboards. We were too frightened to plead. Another century gone to hell—and for what? Just because some people don't know how to bring their children up!

It was the epoch of the masters of levitation.
Some evenings we saw solitary men and women
floating above the dark tree tops. Could they have
been sleeping or thinking? They made no attempt
to navigate. The wind nudged them ever so slightly.
We were afraid to speak, to breathe. Even the
nightbirds were quiet. Later, we'd mention the little
book clasped in the hands of the young woman,
and the way that old man lost his hat to the
cypresses.

In the morning there were not even clouds in
the sky. We saw a few crows preen themselves
at the edge of the road; the shirts raise their empty
sleeves on the blind woman's clothesline.

Ghost stories written as algebraic equations. Little Emily at the blackboard is very frightened. The X's look like a graveyard at night. The teacher wants her to poke among them with a piece of chalk. All the children hold their breath. The white chalk squeaks once among the plus and minus signs, and then it's quiet again.

In the fourth year of the war, Hermes showed up. He was not much to look at. His mailman's coat was in tatters; mice ran in and out of its pockets. The broad-brimmed hat he was wearing had bullet holes. He still carried the famous stick that closes the eyes of the dying, but it looked gnawed. Did he let the dying bite on it? Whatever the case, he had no letters for us. "God of thieves!" we shouted behind his back when he could no longer hear us.

The city had fallen. We came to the window of a house drawn by a madman. The setting sun shone on a few abandoned machines of futility. "I remember," someone said, "how in ancient times one could turn a wolf into a human and then lecture it to one's heart's content."

I PLAYED IN THE
SMALLEST THEATRES

Bits of infernal gravel
On the window sill
Surrounding a solitary
White bread crumb.

The stone is a mirror which works poorly.
Nothing in it but dimness. Your dimness or its dim-
ness, who's to say? In the hush your heart sounds
like a black cricket.

They wheeled out the ash blonde who believes herself already dead into the spike-fenced garden of the hospital for the insane. Her name was Amy or Ann, but she didn't answer to either one. She kept her eyes tightly shut. She was pushed by a nurse in white.

Some of it was told to me by a shivering young man who insisted that it's been raining for years, even indoors. "Coming down real hard," he said.

Lover of endless disappointments with your collection of old postcards, I'm coming! I'm coming! You want to show me a train station with its clock stopped at five past five. We can't see inside the station master's window because of the grime. We don't even know if there's a train waiting on the platform, much less if a woman in black is hurrying through the front door. There are no other people in sight, so it must be a quiet station. Some small town so effaced by time it has only one veiled widow left, and now she too is leaving with her secret.

The flies in the Arctic Circle all come from my sleepless nights. This is how they travel: The wind takes them from butcher to butcher; then the cows' tails get busy at milking time.

At night in the northern woods they listen to the moose, the loon. . . . The summer there is so brief, they barely have time to count their legs.

"Brave as a postage stamp crossing the ocean," they drone and sigh, and already it's time to make snowballs, the little gray ones with stones in them.

HISTORY LESSON

The roaches look like
Comic rustics
In serious dramas.

PART II

The hundred-year-old china doll's head the sea washes up on its gray beach. One would like to know the story. One would like to make it up, make up many stories. It's been so long in the sea, the eyes and nose have been erased, its faint smile is even fainter. With the night coming, one would like to see oneself walking the empty beach and bending down to it.

In a forest of question marks you were no bigger than an asterisk.

O the season of mists! Someone blew the hunting horn.

The dictionary said you were a sign indicating an omission; then it changed the subject abruptly and spoke of "asterisms," which supposedly have to do with crystals showing a starlike luminous figure.

You didn't believe a word of it. The question marks had valentines carved on their trunks so you wouldn't look up and notice the ropes.

Greasy ropes with baby nooses.

Everything's foreseeable. Everything has already been foreseen. What has been fated cannot be avoided. Even this boiled potato. This fork. This chunk of dark bread. This thought too. . . .

My grandmother sweeping the sidewalk knows that. She says there's no god, only an eye here and there that sees clearly. The neighbors are too busy watching TV to burn her as a witch.

He calls one dog Rimbaud and the other Hölderlin. They are both mongrels. "The unexamined life is not worth living" is his favorite saying. His wife looks like Delacroix's half-naked *Liberty*. She wears cowboy boots, picks dangerous-looking mushrooms in the forest. Tonight they will light tall candles and drink wine. Later, they'll open the door for the dogs to come in and eat the scraps under the table. "Entrez, mes enfants!" he'll shout into the night, bowing deeply from the waist.

A dog with a soul, you've got that? You apes with heads of Socrates, false priests' altar boys, retired professors of evil! I imagine cities so I can get lost in them. I meet other dogs with souls when I'm not lighting firecrackers in heads that are about to doze off.

Blood-and-guts firecrackers. In the dark to see, you ass-scratchers! In the dark to see.

Time—the lizard in the sunlight. It doesn't move, but its eyes are wide open. *They love to gaze into our faces and hearken to our discourse.*

It's because the very first men were lizards. If you don't believe me, go grab one by the tail and see it come right off.

Margaret was copying a recipe for "saints roasted with onions" from an old cook book. The ten thousand sounds of the world were hushed so we could hear the scratchings of her pen. The saint was asleep in the bedroom with a wet cloth over his eyes. Outside the window, the author of the book sat in a flowering apple tree killing lice between his fingernails.

A poem about sitting on a New York rooftop
on a chill autumn evening, drinking red wine,
surrounded by tall buildings, the little kids running
dangerously to the edge, the beautiful girl every-
one's secretly in love with sitting by herself. She
will die young but we don't know that yet. She has
a hole in her black stocking, big toe showing,
toe painted red . . . And the skyscrapers . . . in the
failing light . . . like new Chaldeans, pythonesses,
Cassandras . . . because of their many blind
windows.

Dear Friedrich, the world's still false, cruel and beautiful. . . .

Earlier tonight, I watched the Chinese laundryman, who doesn't read or write our language, turn the pages of a book left behind by a customer in a hurry. That made me happy. I wanted it to be a dreambook, or a volume of foolishly sentimental verses, but I didn't look closely.

It's almost midnight now, and his light is still on. He has a daughter who brings him dinner, who wears short skirts and walks with long strides. She's late, very late, so he has stopped ironing and watches the street.

If not for the two of us, there'd be only spiders hanging their webs between the street lights and the dark trees.

"Tropical luxuriance around the idea of the soul," writes Nietzsche. I always felt that, too, Friedrich! The Amazon jungle with its brightly colored birds squawking, squawking, but its depths dark and hushed. The beautiful lost girl is giving suck to a little monkey. The lizards in attendance wear ecclesiastical robes and speak French to her: "La Reine des Reines," they intone. Not the least charm of this tableau is that it can be so easily dismissed as preposterous.

The clouds told him their names in the quiet of the summer afternoon. But when he asked the evening clouds, "Have you seen Mary and Priscilla?," he got no reply. This was a dour and mute bunch. They turned their gray backs on him and drifted over toward Sturgis, where a farmer had just shot a sick horse.

Are Russian cannibals worse than the English? Of course. The English eat only the feet, the Russians the soul. "The soul is a mirage," I told Anna Alexandrovna, but she went on eating mine anyway.

"Like a superb confit of duck, or like a sparkling littleneck clam still in its native brine?" I inquired. But she just rubbed her belly and smiled at me from across the table.

An actor pretending to eat on the stage of the empty theater. The woman who rushes in from the wings has forgotten her lines. O palace bathed in moonlight! The wild-haired woman with her mouth open; the false Prince reaching for his toy pistol.

The dead man steps down from the scaffold.
He holds his bloody head under his arm.

The apple trees are in flower. He's making his
way to the village tavern with everybody watching.
There, he takes a seat at one of the tables and
orders two beers, one for him and one for his head.
My mother wipes her hands on her apron and
serves him.

It's so quiet in the world. One can hear the old
river, which in its confusion sometimes forgets and
flows backwards.

My guardian angel is afraid of the dark. He pretends he's not, sends me ahead, tells me he'll be along in a moment. Pretty soon I can't see a thing. "This must be the darkest corner of heaven," someone whispers behind my back. It turns out her guardian angel is missing too. "It's an outrage," I tell her. "The dirty little cowards leaving us all alone," she whispers. And of course, for all we know, I might be a hundred years old already, and she just a sleepy little girl with glasses.

The dog went to dancing school. The dog's owner sniffed vials of Viennese air. One day the two heard the new Master of the Universe pass their door with a heavy step. After that, the man exchanged clothes with his dog. It was a dog on two legs, wearing a tuxedo, that they led to the edge of the common grave. As for the man, blind and deaf as he came to be, he still wags his tail at the approach of a stranger.

Things were not as black as somebody painted them. There was a pretty child dressed in black and playing with two black apples. It was either a girl dressed as a boy, or a boy dressed as a girl. Whatever, it had small white teeth. The landscape outside its window had been blackened with a heavy and coarse paint brush. It was all very teleological, except when the child stuck out its red tongue.

A hen larger than the barn pecking the other chickens as if they were kernels of white corn. The legend says it's my great-grandmother. We are running for our lives, my great-grandfather leading the way. "We'll take your glasses away, Cornelia," he yells over his shoulder!

She gobbled us all up anyway. It was like what Jonah went through inside the whale, except for the young village bride we met there. She smiled mysteriously in welcome and showed us the beds where we were going to spend our long captivity.

"You'd better stop this nonsense, my dear," we heard our great-grandfather whisper before we fell asleep.

The old farmer in overalls hanging from a barn
beam. The cows looking sideways. The old woman
kneeling under his swaying feet in her Sunday black
dress and touching the ground with her forehead
like a Mohammedan. Outside the sky is full of
sudsy clouds above an endless plowed field with no
other landmarks in view.

The rat kept lovebirds. The window was open. The birds were naked. They shivered in the bright sunlight that fell in the cage.

"It's their nature," said the rat, "to work only at loving and being loved!"

The crucified Jesus agreed. He looked soulful despite the crossed eyes and Mexican bandit moustaches someone had drawn on him.

O witches, O poverty! The two who with a sidelong glance measured the thinness of my neck through the bars of the birdcage I carried on my shoulder . . .

They were far too young and elegant to be storybook witches. They wore low-cut party dresses, black seams in their stockings, lips thickly painted red.

The big-hearted trees offered their leaves by whispering armfuls over the winding path where the two eventually vanished.

I was left with my cage, its immense heaviness, its idiotic feeding dish, the even more absurd vanity mirror, and the faintly sounding silver bell.

Once I knew, then I forgot. It was as if I had fallen asleep in a field only to discover at waking that a grove of trees had grown up around me.

"Doubt nothing, believe everything," was my friend's idea of metaphysics, although his brother ran away with his wife. He still bought her a rose every day, sat in the empty house for the next twenty years talking to her about the weather.

I was already dozing off in the shade, dreaming that the rustling trees were my many selves explaining themselves all at the same time so that I could not make out a single word. My life was a beautiful mystery on the verge of understanding, always on the verge! Think of it!

My friend's empty house with every one of its windows lit. The dark trees multiplying all around it.

The ideal spectator who lives only for art, hands folded behind his back. A blank canvas appropriately entitled "Blank" before him. It's exactly 11 A.M. in the provincial museum. One can hear the rumbling stomach of the uniformed guard, who has the face of someone drowned by moonlight.

Thousands of old men with pants lowered
sleeping in public rest rooms. You're exaggerating!
You're raving! Thousands of Marias, of Magdelenas
at their feet weeping.

My thumb is embarking on a great adventure. "Don't go, please," say the fingers. They try to hold him down. Here comes a black limousine with a veiled woman in the back seat, but no one at the wheel. When it stops, she takes a pair of gold scissors out of her purse and snips the thumb off. We are off to Chicago with her using the bloody stump of my thumb to paint her lips.

GOSPEL

Half-way to nowhere—

I thought I heard
Church bells ringing,
The blind man on the corner
Call out my name.

PART III

PART III

M.

I went on foot to M.
There was no one in M.

I had to tread softly
Past the house of cards—
A whole row of them
Thinking of falling down

In M. at the break of day.

A century of gathering clouds. Ghost ships arriving and leaving. The sea deeper, vaster. The parrot in the bamboo cage spoke several languages. The captain in the daguerreotype had his cheeks painted red. He brought a half-naked girl from the tropics whom they kept chained in the attic even after his death. At night she made sounds that could have been singing. The captain told of a race of men without mouths who subsisted only on scents of flowers. This made his wife and mother say a prayer for the salvation of all unbaptized souls. Once, however, we caught the captain taking off his beard. It was false! Under it he had another beard equally absurd looking.

It was the age of busy widow's walks. The dead languages of love were still in use, but also much silence, much soundless screaming at the top of the lungs.

A black child wore the mask of comedy on
a street of gutted, gray-brick tenements. The mask
came from the ruins of the movie palace where it
had hung over the proscenium with its companion,
tragedy. O child in red sneakers, running. . . . One
expected to see one of the shadowy beauties of the
silent screen sleepwalking in your wake.

Police dogs in a dog groomer's window dressed as children. O the starched white pinafores, the lace-bordered undies, the patent-leather shoes! If you're going to sell your soul to the devil, go down that street and ask on the second floor of the house with the dogs.

Ambiguity created by a growing uncertainty of antecedents bade us welcome.

"The Art of Making Gods" is what the advertisement said. We were given buckets of mud and shown a star atlas. "The Minotaur doesn't like whistling," someone whispered, so we resumed our work in silence.

Evening classes. The sky like a mirror of a dead beauty to use as a model. The spit of melancholia's plague carrier to make it stick.

The time of minor poets is coming. Good-by Whitman, Dickinson, Frost. Welcome you whose fame will never reach beyond your closest family, and perhaps one or two good friends gathered after dinner over a jug of fierce red wine . . . while the children are falling asleep and complaining about the noise you're making as you rummage through the closets for your old poems, afraid your wife might've thrown them out with last spring's cleaning.

It's snowing, says someone who has peeked into the dark night, and then he, too, turns towards you as you prepare yourself to read, in a manner somewhat theatrical and with a face turning red, the long rambling love poem whose final stanza (unknown to you) is hopelessly missing.

—*After Aleksandar Ristović*

At least four or five Hamlets on this block alone. Identical Hamlets holding identical monkey-faced spinning toys.

Comedy of errors at an elegant downtown restaurant.

The chair is really a table making fun of itself. The coat tree has just learned to tip waiters. A shoe is served a plate of black caviar.

"My dear and most esteemed sir," says a potted palm to a mirror, "it is absolutely useless to excite yourself."

The fat man who runs behind her on the street, pleading. Who calls her name . . . says he wants her back! The beautiful black transvestite in a debutante's white satin gown, who fans herself with a newspaper despite the snow on the sidewalk. The people turning to look. The lover with a shaved head, no shoes on his feet, calling on God to witness.

A week-long holiday in a glass paperweight bought at Coney Island. The old lady wipes off the dust every day. I call her an "old lady," but actually she looks like a monkey when she peers into the glass. We wear no clothes, of course. I'm getting a fantastic tan and so is my wife. At night there's a bit of light coming from the aquarium. We turn green. My wife is a wild fern with voluptuously trembling leaves. In goldfish heaven there's peace and calm.

Lots of people around here have been taken for rides in UFOs. You wouldn't think that possible with all the pretty white churches in sight so well-attended on Sundays.

"The round square doesn't exist," says the teacher to the dull-witted boy. His mother was abducted only last night. All expectations to the contrary, she sits in the corner grinning to herself. The sky is vast and blue.

"They're so small, they can sleep inside their own ears," says one eighty-year-old twin to the other.

O the great God of Theory, he's just a pencil stub, a chewed stub with a worn eraser at the end of a huge scribble.

I knew a night owl who dreamed of being a star of country music. O cruel fate! O vale of tears! We drank whiskey in coffee cups in late-hour dives while the juke box spinned her favorites. She fed me forked pieces of steak while my hand strayed under the table. The choirboy counterman's big ears turned crimson. She, with eyes veiled, head thrown back, so that my next bite hung in midair. I had to stretch my neck all the way to take a nibble.

What was I to do? The madness of it was so appealing, and the night so cold.

My father loved the strange books of André Breton. He'd raise the wine glass and toast those far-off evenings "when butterflies formed a single uncut ribbon." Or we'd go out for a piss in the back alley and he'd say: "Here are some binoculars for blindfolded eyes." We lived in a rundown tenement that smelled of old people and their pets.

"Hovering on the edge of the abyss, permeated with the perfume of the forbidden," we'd take turns cutting the smoked sausage on the table. "I love America," he'd tell us. We were going to make a million dollars manufacturing objects we had seen in dreams that night.

An arctic voyager with a room to cross. A large white room spectrally bright and speckless in the morning sunlight.

Far-off kitchen noises . . . If only he could impersonate the look of a stranger arriving on foot in a remote, snowbound region, its sky dazzlingly empty and blue.

It was quiet in the room. He could feel the pins and needles in his new black suit as he waited for the arctic seamstress, the zero on the tip of her tongue.

All this gets us Nowhere—which is a town like any other. The salesgirls of Nowhere are going home at the end of the day. I must assure myself of their reality by begging one for a dime. She obliges and even gives me a little peck on the forehead. I'm ready to throw aside my crutches and walk, but another wags her finger at me and tells me to behave myself.

From inside the pot on the stove someone
threatens the stars with a wooden spoon.

Otherwise, cloudless calm. The shepherd's
hour.

Where ignorance is bliss, where one lies at night on the bed of stupidity, where one prays on one's knees to a foolish angel . . . Where one follows a numbskull to war in an army of beatific dunces . . . Where the roosters crow all day. . . .

The lovely emptyhead is singing the same snatch of a love song over and over. For breakfast on the terrace we are having some eye-fooling painted grapes which even the birds peck at. And now the kisses . . . for which we forgot to remove our Halloween masks.

He had mixed up the characters in the long novel he was writing. He forgot who they were and what they did. A dead woman reappeared when it was time for dinner. A door-to-door salesman emerged out of a backwoods trailer wearing Chinese robes. The day the murderer was supposed to be electrocuted, he was buying flowers for a certain Rita, who turned out to be a ten-year-old girl with thick glasses and braids. . . . And so it went.

He never did anything for me, though. I kept growing older and grumpier, as I was supposed to, in a ratty little town which he always described as "dead" and "near nothing."

Someone shuffles by my door muttering: "Our goose is cooked."

Strange! I have my knife and fork ready. I even have the napkin tied around my neck, but the plate before me is still empty.

Nevertheless, someone continues to mutter outside my door regarding a certain hypothetical, allegedly cooked goose that he claims is ours in common.

A much dwindled, starker annotator sitting in a child's prison for butterflies. There's Phoebus. There's Painted Lady, Dog Face, White Admiral, Zebra, Mourning Cloak, Question Mark, Little Wood Satyr. Their colors are very pretty.

Who told the little kid about sticking pins into us?

MY SECRET IDENTITY IS

The room is empty,
And the window is open

The Book of Gods and Devils

Hotel Insomnia

Unending Blues

A Wedding in Hell

The World Doesn't End